The BIG Orange Book of Beginner Books

By Dr. Seuss

The BIG Orange Book of Beginner Books

By
Dr. Seuss

Illustrated by Dr. Seuss,
Roy McKie, Scott Nash,
and Michael Frith

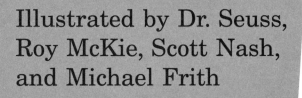

Random House
New York

Dr. Seuss's real name was Theodor Geisel. On books he wrote to be illustrated by others, he often used the name Theo. LeSieg, which is Geisel spelled backward. Rosetta Stone is the name he used for the book Because a Little Bug Went Ka-Choo!, *which he co-wrote with Michael Frith.*

Visit us on the Web!
Seussville.com
randomhousekids.com

Educators and librarians, for a variety of teaching tools, visit us at
RHTeachersLibrarians.com

ISBN: 978-0-553-52425-3
Library of Congress Control Number: 2014948995

Printed in the United States of America   10 9 8 7 6 5 4 3
First Edition

Contents

Marvin K. Mooney Will you PLEASE GO NOW!

By Dr. Seuss

The
time
has come.

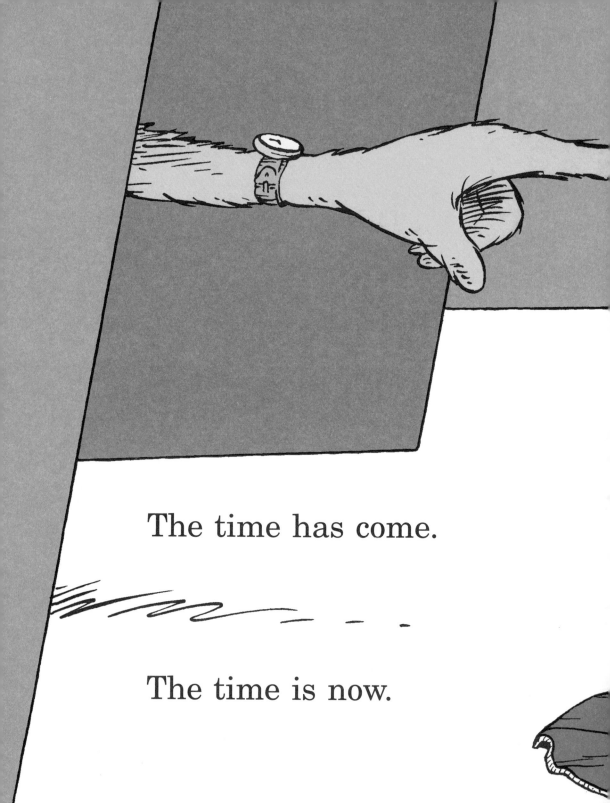

The time has come.

The time is now.

Just go.
Go.
GO!
I don't care how.

You can go by foot.

You can go
by cow.

Marvin K. Mooney,
will you
please go now!

You can go
on skates.

You can go
on skis.

You can go
in a hat.

But
please go.
Please!

I don't care.
You can go
by bike.

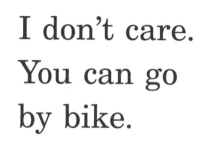

You can go
on a Zike-Bike
if you like.

If you like
you can go
in an old blue shoe.

Just go, go, GO!
Please do, do, DO!

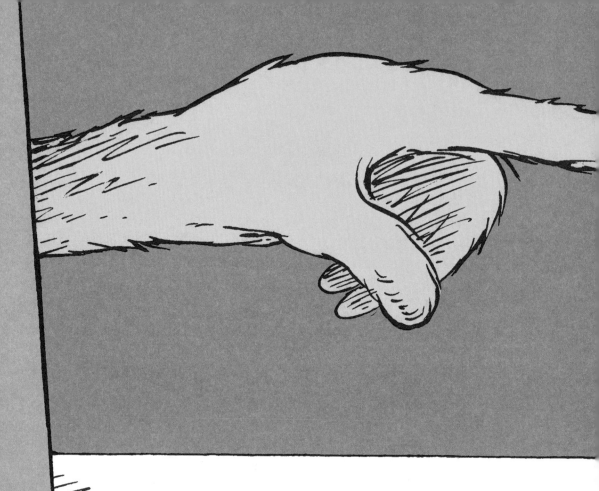

Marvin K. Mooney,
I don't care how.
Marvin K. Mooney,
will you please
GO NOW!

You can go on stilts.

You can go by fish.

You can go
in a Crunk-Car
if you wish.

If you wish
you may go
by lion's tail.

Or stamp yourself
and go by mail.

Marvin K. Mooney!
Don't you know
the time has come
to go, Go, GO!

Get on your way!
Please, Marvin K.!
You might like going
in a Zumble-Zay.

You can go
by balloon . . .

. . . or broomstick.

OR
You can go
by camel
in a
bureau drawer.

You can go by Bumble-Boat . . .

. . . or jet.

I don't care
how you go.
Just GET!

Get yourself a Ga-Zoom.
You can go with a . . . .

Marvin, Marvin, Marvin!
Will you leave this room!

Marvin K. Mooney!
I don't care HOW.

Marvin K. Mooney!

Will you please

GO NOW!

I said

GO

and

GO

I meant. . . .

The time had come.
SO . . .
Marvin WENT.

The SHAPE of ME and OTHER STUFF

By Dr. Seuss

You know . . .

It makes a fellow think.

The shape of you

the
shape
of
me

the shape
of everything I see . . .

a bug . . .

a balloon

a bed

a bike.

No shapes are ever quite alike.

Just think about
the shape of beans

and flowers

and mice

and big machines!

Just think about
the shape of strings

and elephants ....

. . . . .and other things.

The shape of lips.

The shape of ships.

The shape
of water
when
it
drips.

Peanuts

and

pineapples

noses

and

grapes.

Everything
comes
in different shapes.

Why, George!
You're RIGHT!

And . . .
think about
the shape of GUM!

The MANY shapes
of chewing gum!

And the shape
of smoke
and
marshmallows
and
fires.

And mountains

and

roosters

and

horses

and

tires!

And the shape of camels ....

..................the shape of bees

and the wonderful
shapes of back door keys!

And the shapes
of spider webs

and clothes!

And,
speaking of shapes,
now just suppose . . . !

Suppose
YOU
were shaped
like these . . .

. . . or those!

. . . or shaped
like a BLOGG!

Or a garden hose!

Of all
the shapes
we MIGHT have been . . .

I say, "HOORAY
for the shapes we're in!"

In A People House

BY Dr. Seuss*

*writing as
Theo. LeSieg

Illustrated by *Roy McKie*

"Come inside, Mr. Bird,"
said the mouse.
"I'll show you what there is
in a People House . . .

A People House
has things like . . .

. . . chairs

things like

roller skates

and stairs.

banana

bathtub

bottles

brooms

That's what you find
in people's rooms.

73

scissors

needle

buttons

thread

74

cup and saucer

pillow

bed

These are doughnuts.

Here's a door.

Come along, I'll show you more.

Here's a
ceiling

here's a floor

piano

peanuts

popcorn

pails

pencil

paper

hammer

nails

79

salt and pepper

goldfish

key

table

telephone

TV

Come on!
Come on!
There's more to see!

81

You'll see a

kitchen sink

in a People House,

a shoe

and a sock

and a clock
said the mouse.

bread and butter

window

wall

toothbrush

hairbrush

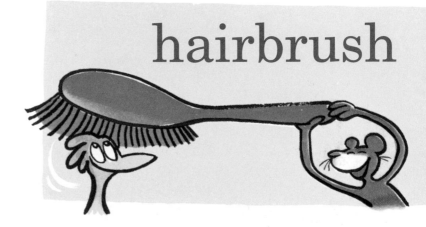

big blue ball

baked beans

bureau drawers

and

books

lights and lamps

and hats and hooks

mirror

marbles

shirt

and string

knife

fork

spoon

and

bells

to

ring

doll
and
dishes

teapot

trash

And . . .
Another thing,
it's time
you knew . . .

. . . A People House
has people, too!

"And now, Mr. Bird,
you know," said the mouse.
"You know what there is
in a People House."

Hooper Humperdink...? NOT HIM!

By Dr. Seuss*

*writing as Theo. LeSieg

Illustrated by Scott Nash

I'm going to have a party.
But I don't think
that I'll ask
Hooper Humperdink.

I'll ask Alice.

I'll ask Abe.

I'll ask Bob
and Bill
and Babe.

I'll ask Charlie, Clara, Cora.
Danny, Davey, Daisy, Dora.

I'll ask Dinny.
I'll ask Dot.

But Hooper Humperdink . . . ?
I'LL NOT!

Elma! Elly! Ethel! Ed!
Frieda, Francis, Frank and Fred.

I'll ask George and Gus and Gary.
Henry, Hedda, Hank and Harry!

I'll ask every kid I like.
Irene, Ivy, Izzy, Ike.
Joe and Jerry, Jack and Jim.

But Hooper Humperdink . . . ?
<u>NOT</u> <u>HIM!</u>

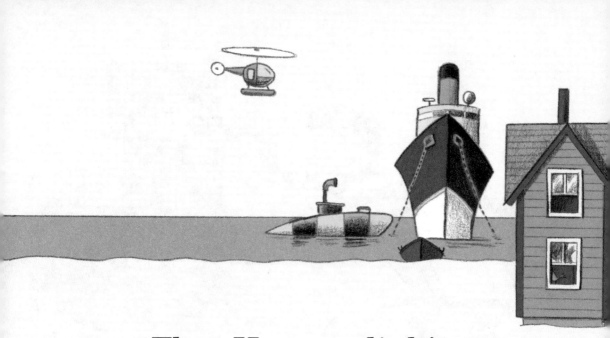

That Humperdink!
I don't know why,
but somehow
I don't like that guy.

A party needs
a band to play.

And so I'll get a band.
O.K.

The K. K. Kats
are on their way!

And I like
Lucy, Luke and Lum.
I like the Lesters.
<u>They</u> can come.

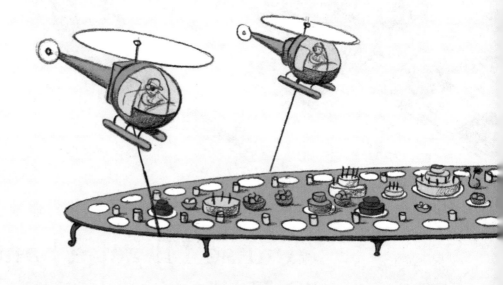

And Mark and Mary!
Mike and Mabel!
I'll have to get
a bigger table!

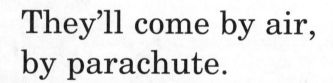

They'll come by air,
by parachute.

Nora,
Norton,
Nat
and Newt!

And Olivetta Oppenbeem!
I'll have to order more ice cream!

I'll need about ten tons,
I think.

But <u>none</u> for
Hooper Humperdink!

No! Humperdink won't do at all.
He's not good fun
like Pete and Paul,
and Pinky, Pat and Pasternack.
I bet they come by camel back.

And so will
lots of other pals,
like the Perkins boys
and the Plimton gals!

Q . . . Q . . . Q . . .
Who begins with "Q"?
Quintuplets!

So I'll ask a few.

Ralph and Rudolf!
Ruth and Russ!

And some other R's
in a big blue bus.

Oh, what a party!
Sally! Sue!
Solly! Sonny!
Steve and Stoo!

I'll ask the Simpson sisters, too.

But
I'm not asking
<u>YOU</u> <u>KNOW</u> <u>WHO</u>!

Nobody
wants to play with Hooper.
Humperdink's a party-pooper!

Welcome, Tim and Tom and Ted!
Grab a hot dog. Get well fed.

Welcome, Ursula! Welcome, Ubb!
Strawberry soda by the tub!

Welcome, Vera!
Violet! Vinny!
Welcome, Wilbur, Waldo,
Winnie!

Xavier!
And Yancy! Yipper!
Zacharias!
Zeke and Zipper!

WELCOME

All my good friends from A to Z!
The biggest gang you'll ever see!
The biggest gang there'll ever be!

A party big and good as this
is too good for <u>anyone</u> to miss!

And so, you know,
    I sort of think . . .

. . . I <u>WILL</u> ask
Hooper Humperdink!

Ten Apples Up On Top!

By
Dr. Seuss*

*Writing as
Theo. LeSieg

Illustrated by
Roy McKie

One apple
up on top!

Two apples
up on top!

Look, you.

I can do it, too.

Look!

See!

I can do three!

Three . . .

Three . . .

I see.

I see.

You can do three
but I can do more.
You have three
but I have four.

Look! See, now.

I can hop

with four apples

up on top.

And I can hop
up on a tree
with four apples
up on me.

Look here, you two.

See here, you two.

I can get five

on top.

Can you?

I am so good

I will not stop.

Five!

Now six!

Now seven on top!

Seven apples
up on top!

I am
so good
they will not drop.

Five, six, seven!
Fun, fun, fun!
Seven, six, five,
four, three, two, one!

But, see!
We are as good as you.
Look! Now we
have seven, too.

And now, see here.

Eight! Eight on top!

Eight apples up!

Not one will drop.

Eight! Eight!

And we can skate.

Look now!

We can skate

with eight.

But I can do nine.
And hop!
And drink!
You can not do this,
I think.

We can! We can!

We can do it, too.

See here.

We are as good as you!

We all are very good,
I think.
With nine, we all
can hop and drink.

170

Nine is very good.

But then . . .

Come on and we

will make it ten!

Look!

Ten

apples

up

on

top!

We are not

going to let them drop!

Look out!

Look out!

I see a mop.

I will make

the apples fall.

Get out. Get out. You!

One and all!

Come on! Come on!
Come down this hall.
We must not let
our apples fall!

Out of our way!

We can not stop.

We can not let

our apples drop.

This is not good.

What will we do?

They want to get

our apples, too.

183

They will get them
if we let them.
Come! We can not
let them get them.

Look out!

The mop!

The mop!

The mop!

You can not stop
our apple fun.
Our apples will not drop.
Not one!

Come on! Come on!

Come one! Come all!

We have to make

the apples fall.

They must not get
our apples down.
Come on! Come on!
Get out of town!

Apples!
Apples up on top!
All of this
must stop
STOP
STOP!

Now all our fun
is going to stop!
Our apples all
are going to drop.

Look!
Ten apples
on us all!

What fun!
We will not
let them fall.

Because a Little Bug went Ka- CHOO!

By
Rosetta Stone

Illustrated by
Michael Frith

You may not believe it,
but here's how it happened.

One fine summer morning . . .

. . . a little bug sneezed.

CHOO!

Because of that sneeze,
a little seed dropped.

Because that seed dropped,
a worm got hit.

Because he got hit,
that worm got mad.

GRRRR

Because he got mad,
he kicked a tree.

Because of that kick,
a coconut dropped.

Because
that nut
dropped,
a turtle
got bopped.

Because he got bopped,
that turtle named Jake
fell on his back
with a splash
in the lake.

Because of that splash,
a hen got wet.

Because she got wet,
that hen got mad.

Because she got mad,
that hen kicked a bucket.

Because of that kick,
the bucket went up.

Because it went up . . .

. . . the bucket
came down.

Because it came down,
it hit Farmer Brown.

And
that
bucket
got
stuck
on
his
head.

Because it got stuck,
Farmer Brown
phoned for help.

Because of his phone call,
policemen came speeding.

Because they were speeding,
they hit a big stone.

And so one policeman
flew up all alone.

Because he flew up . . .

. . . he
had
to
come
down.

And because he came down
on the boat Mary Lou . . .
and because he hit hard . . .

he went right on through.

He made a big hole
in the boat Mary Lou.

Because of that hole,
the boat started to sink.
And because it was sinking . . .
well, what do you think?

Everyone, EVERYONE started to yelp.

And Mrs. Brown called
on the phone for more help.

Because of her phone call,
MORE help came . . . FAST!

They tied a strong rope
to the Mary Lou's mast.

And because of that rope
the boat didn't go down.
But it had to be fixed.
So they started for town.

And because
they went THERE—
it's true, I'm afraid—
they ran right into
a circus parade.

And THAT started something
they'll never forget.

And as far as I know
it is going on yet.

And that's how it happened.

Believe me. It's true.

Because . . .

just because . . .

a small bug

went KA-CHOO!